PETEY the Puppy

by Anne-Marie Dalmais
Illustrated by Annie Bonhomme

English translation
by Diane Cohen

from Aunt Sarah + Uncle Ernie
12/7/89

DERRYDALE BOOKS
New York

Petey is a funny little puppy. He's always dragging around a sturdy wooden cart and in it he carries the strangest things! This morning, he's filled it with a huge stone! "That's certainly heavier than my letters!" the mailman exclaims.

This afternoon Petey has loaded a bunch of reeds into his cart. They are so light that even his little sister, a teensy-weensy puppy who can hardly stand up on her hind paws, pulls them with no trouble at all.

Today, Petey is helping the vegetable seller carry sacks of potatoes from her truck to the back of her store. To thank Petey, she lets him take home a bunch of pretty crates piled unsteadily one on top of the other.

Another day, at the florist's, he
moves flower pots and plants from
the greenhouse to the shop.
In exchange for this small task,
Petey receives a beautiful geranium
in full bloom. He puts it in his
cart right away.

On Sunday, Petey leaves for a long

outing in the nearby forest with

his friend Buddy the Beaver, his

beloved cart, and a hearty snack,

carefully wrapped in a dishcloth.

The two explorers discover four
logs at the edge of a stand of pine
trees.

"We'll take them home," decides
Petey.

So they pull and they push, they
tug and they tow. They yell,
"Heave ho! Heave ho!" and bring
the cart full of logs home.

Even when he's invited to a friend's house for lunch, Petey takes along his cart. He simply can't leave home without it! Uncle Prince and Aunt Lady fill it with nice gifts: some very smooth wooden boards and a thick roll of blue fabric.

But what's Petey the Puppy going
to do with this hodgepodge of
odd objects? What indeed?
For the moment, he stores them
in an open shed with the garden
tools.

For the last few days, Henry the Hedgehog has come to see Petey every afternoon, carrying his toolbox with him. In the back of the garden, near the apple trees, you can hear stange noises: "Tap tap! Tap tap!"

Look what the two friends have
built! It's a funny little hut built
out of all the things Petey
collected!

Petey is so proud of his new
"home." Here he can read or sleep
or dream about future journeys
with his trusty wooden cart.